Build-Your-Own
BIRDHOUSE 1-2-3!

by Kimberly Weinberger • Illustrated by Edward Miller

Cartwheel
·B·O·O·K·S·®

SCHOLASTIC INC.

New York Toronto London Auckland Sydney Mexico City New Delhi Hong Kong

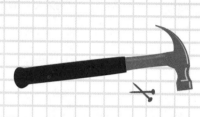

Text written by Kimberly Weinberger.
Illustrations by Edward Miller.
Copyright © 2001 by Homer TLC, Inc. All rights reserved.
Home Depot, The Home Depot, and the Orange Square Logo are registered
trademarks of Homer TLC, Inc.
Published by Scholastic Inc. SCHOLASTIC, CARTWHEEL BOOKS, and associated
logos are trademarks and/or registered trademarks of Scholastic Inc.

ISBN 0-439-29499-1

10 9 8 7 6 5 4 3 2 1   01 02 03 04 05

Printed in the U.S.A.   24
First printing, November 2001

Just as a bird uses its beak as a tool to build a nest, you can use your own tools to help our feathered friends. How? By building a birdhouse!

Birdhouse

Front (A)

Side (C)   Side (D)

Roof (E)   Roof (F)

Back (B)   Dowel   Bottom (G)

A wooden birdhouse is the perfect place for birds to safely nest. And building one is a great project for you and a grown-up to do together.

The first step is to gather all of the materials you'll need. Buy all of the necessary components at The Home Depot®. Or, if you prefer, you can buy a complete Home Depot birdhouse kit with pre-cut, pre-drilled wood and all of the necessary nails and screws at Toys R Us®. If a kit is not available, a grown-up will need to measure and cut the following pieces of wood:

Two five-sided pieces of wood
bottom 5" wide (12.7 cm)
sides 5" (12.7 cm)
upper sides 3 $^1/_2$" (9 cm)
$^3/_4$" thick (1.9 cm)

The front piece of the birdhouse should have a hole drilled all the way through the entire piece of wood. The second piece of wood will be the back of the birdhouse.

The hole should begin 2" (5 cm) from the pointed top of the piece. The hole should be 1 $^1/_4$" (3 cm) wide.

A second, shallow hole should be drilled 1" (2.5 cm) below the first hole. This second hole should not go through the entire piece of wood. The hole should be $^3/_8$" (0.9 cm) wide and $^1/_2$" (1.3 cm) deep.

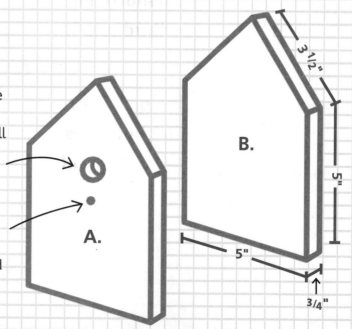

Two pieces of wood

4" x 4" x ⁵/₈"

(10 cm x 10 cm x 1.6 cm)

These pieces will form the sides of your birdhouse.

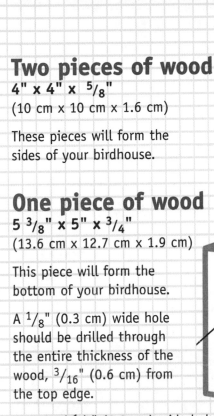

C.

D.

4"

4"

⁵/₈"

One piece of wood

5 ³/₈" x 5" x ³/₄"

(13.6 cm x 12.7 cm x 1.9 cm)

This piece will form the bottom of your birdhouse.

A ¹/₈" (0.3 cm) wide hole should be drilled through the entire thickness of the wood, ³/₁₆" (0.6 cm) from the top edge.

A second ¹/₈" (0.3 cm) wide hole should be drilled through the entire thickness of the wood, ³/₁₆" (0.6 cm) from the bottom edge.

5 ³/₈"

G.

5"

³/₄"

One piece of wood

6 ¹/₄" x 4 ¹/₂" x ³/₄"

(15.8 cm x 11.4 cm x 1.9 cm)

This piece will form the smaller part of the roof.

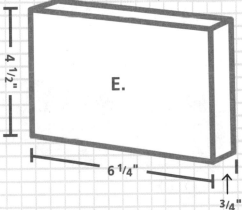

4 ¹/₂"

E.

6 ¹/₄"

³/₄"

One piece of wood

6 ¹/₄" x 5 ¹/₈" x ³/₄"

(15.8 cm x 13 cm x 1.9 cm)

This piece will form the larger part of the roof.

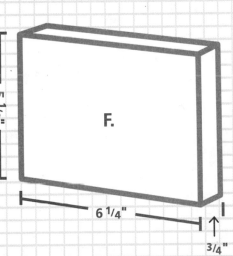

5 ¹/₈"

F.

6 ¹/₄"

³/₄"

One wooden dowel stick

1 ³/₈" long x ³/₈" in diameter

(3.5 cm x 0.9 cm)

A dowel stick is a rounded stick of wood with flat ends. It will be the perch for birds to rest upon.

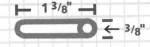

1 ³/₈"

³/₈"

Once you have all of your wood pieces, it's time to collect the rest of your materials and tools. You will need:

Nine 1¼" (3 cm) finish nails

You might want to have a few extra nails on hand as well. Nails can sometimes bend if they're not hammered correctly.

Nail Claw Hammer

Your hammer should have a steel head and a strong handle to grip. One side of the hammer's head should be a V-shaped claw. This side will remove any nails that might bend during hammering.

Two 1¼" (3 cm) long screws

The heads of the screws should be ¼" (0.6 cm) in diameter. They should each have a small **X** on their heads, for use with a Phillips® screwdriver.

Phillips® Screwdriver

When working with a screw that has a small **X** on its head, a Phillips® screwdriver is needed. The tip of this screwdriver is specially made to fit into the screw.

Sandpaper

This is a sheet of paper with fine, medium, or coarse grains of sand covering one side. For this project, a medium-grade sandpaper should be used. Using a sanding block to hold the sandpaper will make the job easier.

Wood Glue

This product usually comes in a plastic squeeze bottle. The glue is specially made to stick to wood surfaces.

Wood Glue

Goggles

When working with tools, you should always wear goggles to protect your eyes.

Safety Rules

You now have all of the materials and tools needed to start building your birdhouse. ***But wait!*** Before you begin, it's important to review the safety rules that are part of any building project.

Always work with an adult.

Tools and materials like hammers and nails can be dangerous if used the wrong way. Never use a tool without a grown-up to watch over you.

1

Wear goggles.

Goggles protect your eyes from flying dust and other dangerous particles.

3. Work on a hard, solid surface.

To hammer wood correctly, you'll need to place your wood pieces on a strong surface for support. Find a sturdy worktable or a hard floor to work on this project.

4. Work slowly and safely.

Pounding the tiny head of a nail can be tricky at first. Rushing may cause your hammer to slip and pound your thumb instead of the nail—*ouch!* Be extra careful and take your time. Your fingers will thank you!

By following all of these safety rules, you'll be an expert in no time. So turn the page and let's start building!

Step 1

- Place the five-sided piece of wood without the holes in front of you. This will be the back of your birdhouse.

- Hammer a nail near the lower left corner of the piece of wood, about $3/8$" (0.9 cm) from the outside edge, until it stands securely on its own. Don't hammer the nail completely! You'll do that job in the next step.

- Place a second nail into the lower right corner of the wood. Repeat the same process, hammering the nail into place so that it stands on its own.

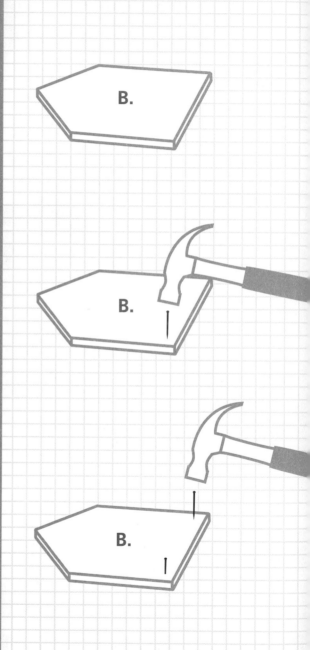

Step 2

- Stand the two 4" x 4" (10 cm x 10 cm) side pieces on their ends.

- Gently place the five-sided back piece, with the nails already in place, on top of the side pieces. The sides and bottom of the back piece should be carefully lined up with both side pieces.

- You are now ready to join the back piece to the side pieces by hammering the two nails completely into the wood.

> After you hammer the first nail into place, remember to line up the sides and back once again. The pounding of the hammer may have caused the pieces to shift.

- Using the same hammering technique, hammer the second nail into place.

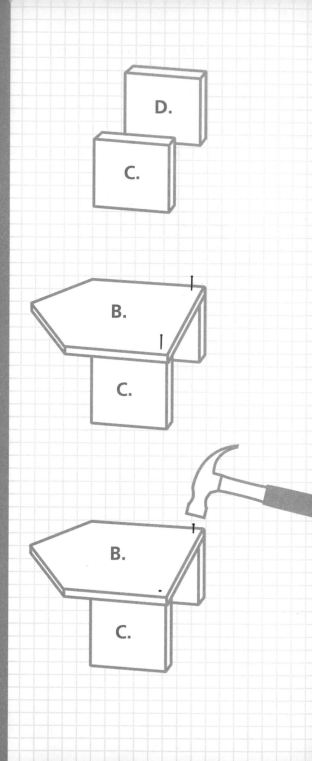

Hammering a nail is not easy. Ask a grown-up to help you. Holding the nail between your thumb and index finger as you hammer will help to guide the nail straight down into the wood. Be sure not to hold the nail too long, or you may hit your fingers with your hammer.

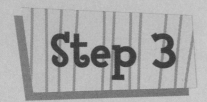

Now that you've connected the back piece to the side pieces, you're ready to move on to the front of your birdhouse.

- Turn the back and side pieces over so that the sides are sticking up.

- Place the five-sided piece of wood, with the holes, on top of the side pieces. The shallow hole on this piece of wood should be faceup. This is the front of your birdhouse.

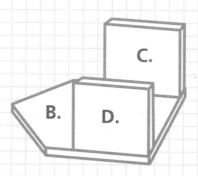

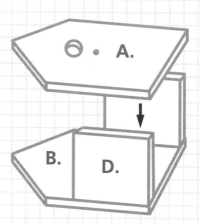

Step 4

- Hold a nail near the left edge of the front piece, about 2 $\frac{1}{4}$" (5.7 cm) from the bottom. Be sure not to position the nail too close to the edge of the wood. Firmly strike the head of the nail with your hammer.

- After hammering, make sure all of the edges are lined up correctly.

- Then hammer a second nail into the right side of the front piece.

You've now joined the front, back, and sides of your birdhouse!

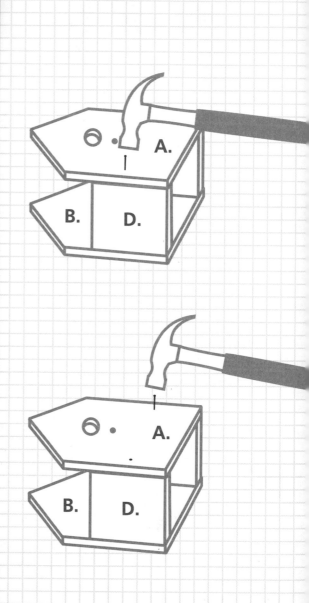

If the nail is not going in straight, use the V-shaped claw side of your hammer to remove it. Hammering takes lots of practice. *Don't give up!*

Step 5

- Place the 5 $\frac{3}{8}$" x 5" x $\frac{3}{4}$" (13.6 cm x 12.7 cm x 1.9 cm) piece of wood so that it lines up correctly with the front, back, and sides. This is the bottom of your birdhouse.

- Lay the assembly on its side.

- Place the tip of a screw in one of the holes in the bottom piece of wood. Using a Phillips® screwdriver, turn the screw clockwise, or to the right, until it tightly joins the two pieces of wood.

- Place the second screw in the other hole. Using the same technique, turn the screw into place.

18

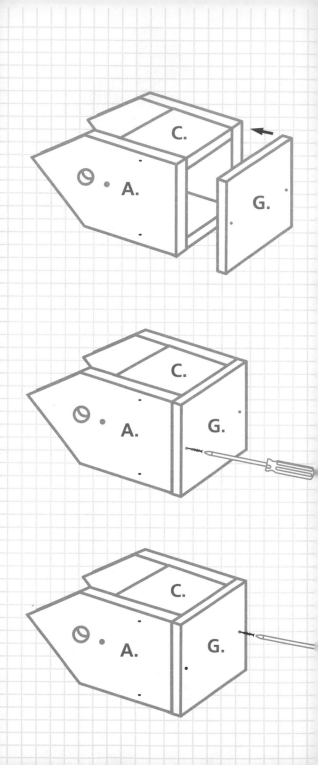

 **Step 6**

You're now ready to attach the final portion of your birdhouse—the roof.

- Lay the assembly on its base.

- Place the 6 $\frac{1}{4}$" x 4 $\frac{1}{2}$" x $\frac{3}{4}$" (15.8 cm x 11.4 cm x 1.9 cm) piece of wood across the top right of the birdhouse. This is the smaller side of the roof. You'll see that the piece is wider than the house itself. This is so that the extra wood can hang over the front entrance to the birdhouse.

- Hold a nail on the left side of the roof piece, about 2" (5 cm) above the bottom edge. Is the nail positioned well? It should join the roof piece with the front of the birdhouse when hammered in place.

- Because the pieces can slip easily, this step calls for two people. Ask a grown-up to hold the roof piece firmly against the rest of the birdhouse while you hammer the nail.

Step 7

- Place the 6 $\frac{1}{4}$" x 5 $\frac{1}{8}$" x $\frac{3}{4}$" (15.8 cm x 13 cm x 1.9 cm) piece of wood across the opening. This is the larger side of the roof. Let the extra wood hang over the front of the house, as the smaller roof piece does.

- Hammer a nail through the top center of the large roof piece so that it joins with the smaller roof piece.

- Next, hold a nail near the right side of the large roof piece, about 2" (5 cm) above the bottom edge. Hammer this nail into place, joining the roof to the front of the house.

- Finally, repeat the same process with the last nail on the left side of the roof.

Step 8

The final piece of wood for your birdhouse is the 1 $\frac{3}{8}$" (3.5 cm) long dowel stick.

- Squeeze a small dot of glue on one end of the stick. Be sure *NOT* to squeeze too hard! Only a small amount of glue is needed.

- Push the glued end of the dowel stick into the small, shallow hole on the front of the birdhouse. This is a perch for the birds to rest upon.

- Press firmly on the dowel stick for a count of five seconds.

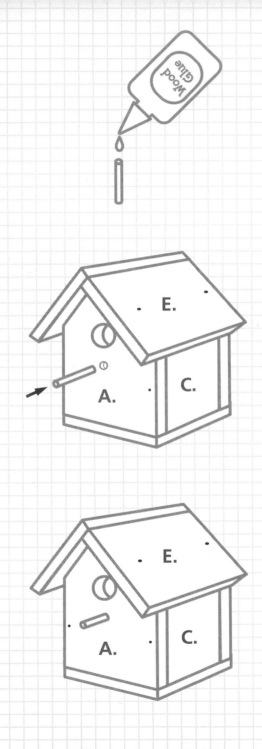

Congratulations!

You've built a birdhouse! Now you're ready for the finishing touches.

Wood Glue

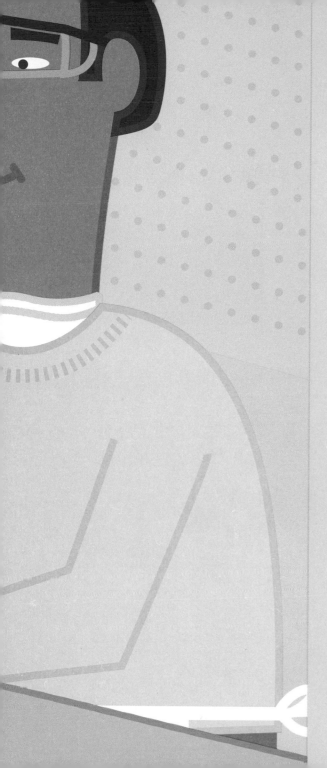

Step 9

- The wood you have been using is probably rough around the edges. To make your birdhouse smooth, gently rub your sandpaper along any splintered spots.

Sandpaper works best when you rub at a steady pace—not too fast, not too slow. Try rubbing in small circles as you go. Before you know it, your birdhouse will be smooth and splinter-free!

This last step is optional. If you like the natural wood of your birdhouse as it is, then you've finished your project. Good job!

If you'd like to decorate your birdhouse, why not add some color? Ask a grown-up to help you paint your birdhouse any color you like. Be sure the paint is completely dry before placing it outside.

Once you've put your birdhouse outside, watch as all types of beautiful birds flock to it. Now the birds will always have a home—right in your own backyard!

THE HOME DEPOT® PROJECT AWARD

_____

(Fill in your name)

successfully built a wooden birdhouse on

.

_____

(Fill in date)